Arnie Lightning

FRANKY THE FROG

Table of Contents

Franky the Frog

Franky the Frog had his nose stuck out of the pond where he lived. He had spent most of the day swimming in the pond. He was sniffing the fresh air above the water and was enjoying it. Franky was very happy.

"Now Franky," said Mother when she saw the nose sticking out of the water. "We are going to be cleaning up the pond today so please stick around the pond and don't go too far away."

"Okay," said Franky. "I won't."

Franky hopped out of the water and walked up the laneway a little ways. He sat on a rock nearby. Just as he did so, his friend, Felix the Fly came along and sat on his nose. Franky tried to flick Felix off his nose with his tongue but Felix was faster than he was.

"Felix, why did you land on my nose?" asked Franky.

"I needed a safe place to land," said Felix. "I was being chased by a nasty lizard."

"You do know that this isn't a very safe place to land," said Franky.

"It is safe enough," said Felix, still avoiding Franky's tongue. "You know you love it when I land on your nose and tickle it."

"You know I don't," said Franky, laughing. "You keep this up and you are going to make me sneeze."

Felix knew that Franky had a wicked sneeze and so he decided he probably better not jump on his nose any more that day.

"Is this better?" asked Felix, jumping up and landing on Franky's forehead.

"Yes," said Franky. "That is much better."

Franky and Felix sat for about an hour talking about what they wanted to do that day.

"I think we should spend the day playing," said Felix. "It is a beautiful day today."

Franky just remembered that he had promised his mother that he would help her clean up the pond.

"Oh dear," said Franky. "I am supposed to be helping Mother clean up the pond today. I am going to be in so much trouble."

"Just tell your mother that you were helping me," said Felix.

"Helping you do what?" asked Franky. "I can't lie to my mother. She knows every time I lie."

"Helping me to stay safe from the nasty lizard," said Felix. "And that wouldn't be a lie."

"Well," said Franky. "That is actually the truth so I can tell her that."

Franky went back to the pond and his mother was already asking about him.

"That Franky," said Mother looking outside for Franky. "He is always late. We have to get this pond cleaned up. It is a mess."

"I am here," said Franky.

"Where were you?" asked Mother.

"I was helping Felix stay safe," said Franky.

"Well that is a very honorable thing to do," said Mother. "I am very proud of you son."

"So does that mean I am forgiven for being late?" said Franky.

"Yes," said Mother, giving Franky a quick hug. "As long as you get to work right away on the pond, I forgive you."

Franky worked hard on cleaning up the pond and Mother was very proud of him for helping others and doing his chores!

Franky the Frog Does a Dance

Franky the Frog was sitting on a lily pad in the middle of the pond where he lived.

"Franky," said Mother. "Don't forget we have a special dinner today."

"Yes," said Franky. "I won't forget."

It was Mother's birthday and she was preparing all her special foods in celebration.

"I am a happy frog," said Franky.

Franky was a very happy frog. It was a beautiful sunny day at the pond and after about a month of nothing but rain, Franky was so happy to bask in the sun.

"Why are so happy today?" asked Franky's friend, Felix the Fly.

"It isn't raining out," said Franky. "That makes me very happy."

"Me too," said Felix. "I did not like all that rain."

"It is easier for me to adapt to the rain," said Franky. "But it must be terrible for you."

"It is," said Felix. "I have to hide under a leaf or rock or fly off to where it isn't raining."

"True," said Franky. "You wouldn't be able to get very wet."

"No," said Felix, suddenly having the urge to spread his wings open and enjoy the cool breeze. "I would not like to get wet at all."

Franky saw Felix spreading his wings and he decided he wanted to do a jig. He got up onto his hind legs on the lily pad and he danced a jig.

"Oh Franky!" exclaimed Felix, deciding he wanted to dance a jig too. "This is so much fun!"

Franky and Felix danced for most of that afternoon. They were pretty tired after all their dancing so they decided to take a nap.

"Franky," Felix heard when he woke up from his nap. "Where are you?"

Felix shook Franky but he was so sound asleep that he couldn't wake him. He decided he would jump up onto his nose. Franky woke with a start and he sneezed, as Felix went flying. Franky quickly stuck out his tongue and caught Felix before he hurt himself.

"Thank you," said Felix. "You and your sneezes are pretty deadly."

"Yes," said Franky, apologetically. "They are but I am glad you weren't hurt."

Felix jumped from Franky's tongue to the top of Franky's head.

"Now," said Franky. "Why did you wake me? I was having a good nap."

"Yes," said Felix. "You were. However, I think your mother is calling you."

"Oh Franky!" exclaimed Mother, her voice getting louder and louder. "Where are you?"

"Oh dear," said Franky, rushing over to where his mother was. "It is time for Mother's birthday dinner."

"You better get going," said Felix.

"Come with me," said Franky. "It isn't like you would eat much."

"Okay," said Felix. "I would enjoy that."

Mother, Franky and Felix enjoyed the birthday meal very much. They were so full afterwards that they could not move. They all needed a nap.

"Do I have any chores to do right now?" asked Franky, hoping that he wouldn't have to wake up by Felix jumping on his nose again.

"No," said Mother. "You are okay for tonight."

Mother, Franky and Felix had a good nap after their delicious meal and Felix did not wake Franky up by jumping on his nose. Instead he woke him up by jumping on his forehead and then slipping and landing on his nose.

Franky the Frog is Upset

Franky the Frog was sitting on a rock enjoying the day. He was very happy that he had the whole day without having to do anything.

"Franky," said Mother. "We need to go shopping today so don't go too far away."

"I thought I didn't have to do anything today," said Franky. "I thought I had the whole day to myself."

"Well," said Mother. "Do you have any plans for today?"

"Not really," said Franky.

"Then come shopping with me," said Mother.

"Oh alright," said Franky. "I will."

Franky wasn't very happy about the fact that he had to go shopping but he didn't mind helping out his mother. He did want to just spend the day with his friend Felix the Fly though.

"We can get together soon," said Felix, when he stopped by later on that morning and seeing his best friend upset.

"But I wanted to play with you today," said Franky.

"I know," said Felix. "But isn't it better to help your mother?"

"Yes," said Franky. "I do suppose."

Franky and Felix played for a little while before Mother came out of the house and wanted to go.

"I will see you later," said Felix.

Franky went to the shopping mall with his mother. They stopped outside of a clothing store.

"What are we doing here?" asked Franky.

"Well," said Mother. "I wanted to surprise you and buy you a new pair of shoes."

"That would be so nice," said Franky.

"Yes," said Mother. "I have been saving money so I can do this for you."

Franky was so happy. He had been wanting a new pair of shoes.

"Now I will be able to dance better," said Franky.

"Yes," said Mother. "That will be nice."

Franky and Mother picked out a pair of black leather shoes that fit Franky just right and looked really nice on him.

"These shoes are perfect," said Franky, once Mother had paid for them.

Franky wore his shoes home from the store and he would randomly break out in a little dance with them. He met up with Felix later that day and Felix liked his new shoes.

"Look how good you can dance now," said Felix.

"Yes," said Franky. "Isn't it amazing?"

"It sure is," said Felix. "I am glad to see you aren't upset anymore."

"I am very happy again," said Franky.

"Good," said Felix. "Let's go play."

"I can play with you," said Franky. "However I don't want to get my new shoes dirty."

"Well," said Felix. "We can dance then."

Franky and Felix danced the afternoon away. They had so much fun.

"Thank you for my new shoes," said Franky to his mother later that day.

"You are welcome," said Mother. "I am glad you like them."

Franky the Frog and Felix the Fly

Franky the Frog was thinking about what he wanted to do for the day when his friend, Felix the Fly came along and landed on his nose.

"Achoo!!!" said Franky, sneezing.

"Why do you always land on my nose?" asked Franky. "You know that tickles and it makes me sneeze."

Franky saw that Felix was going to hit his head on a tree branch because of the force of his sneeze. Franky stuck out his tongue and caught Felix just in time.

"Oh my!" exclaimed a nasty lizard in the pond. "Franky is going to eat Felix for dinner."

"No," said Franky. "I would never do that to Felix. He is my friend. I care about him too much to do that."

"I see," said the nasty lizard, rolling his eyes toward Felix.

"Don't you dare think you are going to hurt Felix!" exclaimed Franky, coming between Felix and the nasty lizard.

The nasty lizard slithered away but kept his eyes on Felix the whole time.

"You are going to have to be very careful of that nasty lizard," said Franky.

"You are so nice to me," said Felix. "You stuck up for me."

"I am your friend," said Franky. "I am not going to let anything bad happen to you."

"I would do the same for you," said Felix.

The next day, Franky and Felix were outside at the pond. They were dancing and having fun.

"It is such a fun day," said Franky, laughing and singing.

"Oh yes," said Felix. "It certainly is."

Felix saw a bird flying around above Franky's head and it appeared that the bird was just getting ready to swoop down toward Franky. Felix knew he had to do something because he was not going to let the bird hurt his friend.

Felix flew up to the bird as close as he could get. He flew into the bird's right eye. The bird had a difficult time seeing and was diverted from trying to swoop down on Franky.

"Get out of my eye!" exclaimed the bird.

"Do you promise to leave my friend alone?" asked Felix.

"Okay," said the bird. "I promise."

Franky was sitting on the lily pad watching the whole ordeal and was amazed that Felix did so much for him.

"You do know that you just saved my life," said Franky.

"Yes," said Felix. "I told you I would help you."

"Thank you," said Franky. "I think we have a one of a kind relationship. We care about each other enough to save each other's lives."

"Yes," said Felix. "We do. I think that means we are true friends."

"We sure are," said Franky, wiping a tear from his eyes.

Franky and Felix always looked out for each other. They helped each other through thick and thin and if one was going to be hurt they were there to help the other out.

Franky the Frog is Very Happy

Franky the Frog was sitting talking to his best friend, Felix the Fly. They were talking about how they were so happy to be friends with one another and how happy that they lived in the pond they lived in.

"I am so happy," said Franky.

"I am too," said Felix.

"I think we need to sing and dance," said Franky.

"Good idea," said Felix.

Mother came out to talk to Franky and she enjoyed watching the two friends dancing and singing. She joined in with them.

"Oh Mother!" exclaimed Franky. "I am so happy!"

"Oh me too!" exclaimed Mother.

"Happy, happy," sang Franky. "Hoppy, hoppy!"

Franky was hopping around from one lily pad to another having a grand time. He even slipped off one lily pad and ended up in the pond. Felix and Mother turned and saw Franky swimming in the water. They both helped him out of the water and to get back onto the lily pad.

"Oh dear," said Mother about an hour later. "Franky, I came out here to ask you and Felix if you wanted a snack."

"Oh," said Franky. "I don't think so. I am having too much fun."

"Me too," said Felix.

Mother went inside and came out about ten minutes later with two ice cream cones in her hand.

"Here," said Mother. "You can still have fun and eat ice cream too!"

Franky and Felix both enjoyed their ice cream cones and they both were very relieved that Mother did bring them one.

"That was very good ice cream," said Felix. "Thank you!"

"You are very welcome," said Mother.

"It was delicious," said Franky. "And it cooled me down. I was so hot from dancing and singing."

"Me too!" exclaimed Felix.

Franky and Felix were refreshed enough to sing and dance some more. They were having so much fun. Mother couldn't help but join in again with them.

"Oh dear," said Mother a little while later.

"What is the matter?" asked Franky.

"I am having so much fun," said Mother.

"That is good," said Franky. "Having fun is not a bad thing, is it?"

"Oh no," said Mother. "Quite the opposite. However, I forgot to start cooking dinner."

"Oh," said Franky. "Well, why don't Felix and I help you with dinner after we are finished dancing and having fun."

"Okay," said Mother. "That is a deal. I would like that!"

Franky and Felix washed the vegetables and helped chop them while Mother made a homemade salad dressing. Franky and Felix did such a good job with the vegetables and helping her out in the kitchen with dinner that she gave them another scoop of ice cream after dinner.

"Oh this tastes so good," said Franky.

"Yes," said Felix, enjoying it as well. "Thank you!"

Funny Frog Jokes

Q: Why was the frog sad?

A: He was unhoppy!

Q: What kind of shoes do frogs like?

A: Open toad sandals!

Q: What do you get if you mix a toad and a dog?

A: A croaker spaniel!

Q: What do toads like to drink?

A: Croaka-cola!

Q: How come the frog cannot weigh itself?

A: It has no scales!

Q: What do frogs drink on a cold day?

A: Hot croako!

Q: What job did the frog sign up for?

A: Fly catcher!

Q: What do you call a rich frog?

A: A gold-blooded toad.

Q: What do you say to a hitch hiking frog?

A: Hop in!

Q: Why are frogs so happy?

A: They eat whatever bugs them!

Q: What does a frog say when it washes car windows?

A: Rub it, rub it, rub it!

Q: What do you get if mix a frog with some mist?

A: Kermit the Fog!

Q: What do you call a 100 year old frog?

A: An old croak!

Q: What do you say if you meet a toad?

A: Warts new buddy?

Q: What did one frog say to the other?

A: Time sure is fun when you are having flies!

Q: What is a toad's favorite candy?

A: Lollihops!

Maze 1

Can you find your way through the maze?

Maze 2

Can you find your way through the maze?

Maze 3

Can you find your way through the maze?

Maze 4

Can you find your way through the maze?

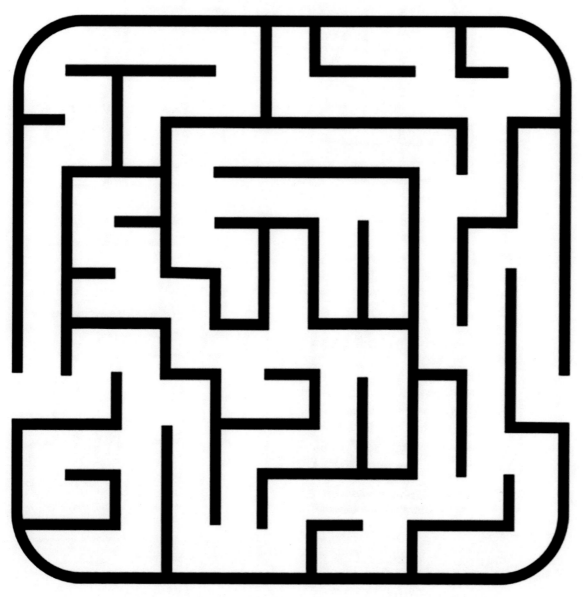

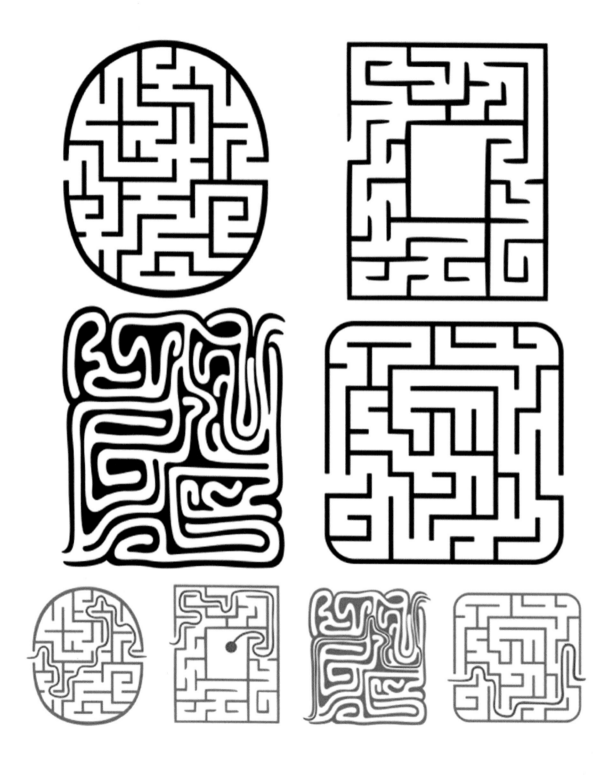

You will also enjoy...

About the Author

Arnie Lightning is a dreamer. He believes that everyone should dream big and not be afraid to take chances to make their dreams come true. Arnie enjoys writing, reading, doodling, and traveling. In his free time, he likes to play video games and run. Arnie lives in Mississippi where he graduated from The University of Southern Mississippi in Hattiesburg, MS.

For more books by Arnie Lightning, please visit:

www.ArnieLightning.com

Made in the USA
San Bernardino, CA
04 September 2016